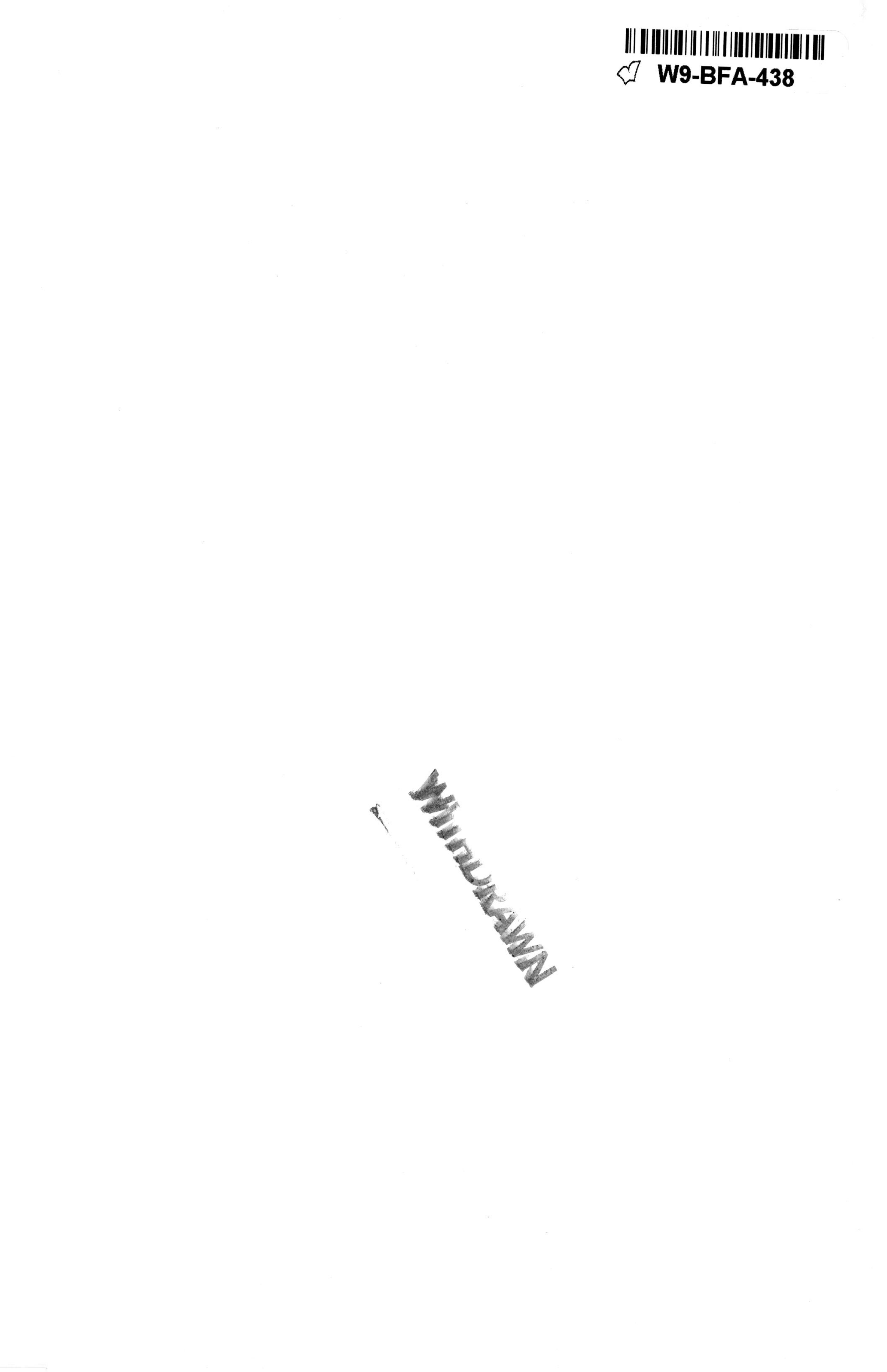
W9-BFA-438
WITHDRAWN

FAIRY TALE DESSERTS

A COOKBOOK FOR YOUNG READERS AND EATERS

Fairy Tales retold by

Jane Yolen

Recipes by

Heidi E.Y. Stemple

Illustrations by

Philippe Béha

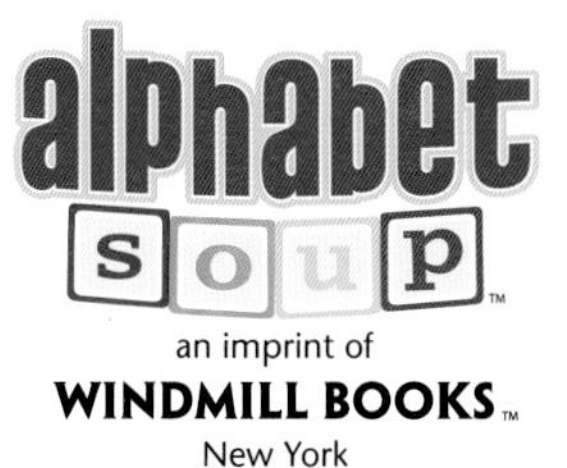

an imprint of
WINDMILL BOOKS™
New York

For my daughter, for meals cooked, jokes shared, and love always
–JY

For Jen and the thousands of dinners we cooked together, for Nina whose name should be on this book for all the help she gave me, and for all my taste testers especially my daughters–Maddison and Glendon
–HEYS

For my daughters Sara and Fanny
–PB

The recipes in this book are intended to be prepared with an adult's help.

Published in 2010 by Windmill Books, LLC
303 Park Avenue South, Suite # 1280, New York, NY 10010-3657

Adapted from *Fairy Tale Feasts: A Literary Cookbook for Young Readers and Eaters.*
Published by arrangement with Crocodile Books, an imprint of Interlink Publishing Group, Inc.

Publisher Cataloging Data

Yolen, Jane

Fairy tale desserts : a cookbook for young readers and eaters. – School & library ed. / fairy tales retold by Jane Yolen ; recipes by Heidi E. Y. Stemple ; illustrations by Philippe Béha.

p. cm. – (Fairy tale cookbooks)

Contents: Cinderella–The magic pear tree–Snow White.

Summary: This book includes retellings of three fairy tales paired with dessert recipes connected to each story.

ISBN 978-1-60754-583-5 (lib.) – ISBN 978-1-60754-584-2 (pbk.)
ISBN 978-1-60754-585-9 (6-pack)

1. Cookery–Juvenile literature 2. Desserts–Juvenile literature 3. Fairy tales [1. Cookery 2. Desserts 3. Fairy tales] I. Stemple, Heidi E. Y. II. Béha, Philippe III. Title IV. Series

641.5/123–dc22

Manufactured in the United States of America.

TABLE OF CONTENTS

STORIES AND STOVETOPS:
AN INTRODUCTION 4

CINDERELLA 7
Pumpkin Tartlets 12

THE MAGIC PEAR TREE 15
Magic Pear Grumble 18

SNOW WHITE 21
Snow White's Baked Apples 30

Stories and Stovetops: An Introduction

From the earliest days of stories, when hunters came home from the hunt to tell of their exploits around the campfire while gnawing on a leg of beast, to the era of kings in castles listening to the storyteller at the royal dinner feast, to the time of TV dinners when whole families gathered to eat and watch movies together, stories and eating have been close companions.

So it is not unusual that folk stories are often about food: Jack's milk cow traded for beans, Snow White given a poisoned apple, a pancake running away from those who would eat it.

But there is something more–and this is about the powerful ties between stories and recipes. Both are changeable, suiting the need of the maker and the consumer.

A storyteller never tells the same story twice, because every audience needs a slightly different story, depending upon the season or the time of day, the restlessness of the youngest listener, or how appropriate a tale is to what has just happened in the storyteller's world. And every cook knows that a recipe changes according to the time of day, the weather, the altitude, the number of grains in the level teaspoonful, the ingredients found (or not found) in the cupboard or refrigerator, the tastes or allergies of the dinner guests, even the cook's own feelings about the look of the batter.

So if you want to tell these stories yourself or make these recipes yourself, be playful. After first making them exactly as they are in this book, you can begin to experiment. Recipes, like stories, are made more beautiful by what *you* add to them. Add, subtract, change, try new ways. We have, and we expect you will, too. In fact, in the recipes, we have already given you some alternatives, like different toppings and other spices.

–Jane Yolen and Heidi E. Y. Stemple

Cinderella

Once there was a man of some property and means whose wife had died, leaving him with a young daughter named Ella.

Believing the child needed a mother to raise her, he married soon after, a woman with two daughters of her own. But hardly were the wedding vows spoken then the new wife began to show her bad temper. She made Ella clean the dishes and mop the floors and do all the work in the house. Ella was even thrown out of her own bedroom and given a straw pallet in the attic. If her father noticed anything, he said nothing for he was ruled entirely by his new wife.

Each day, after she had finished her many chores, little Ella would sit and sigh by the fire, where her clothes became dirty with the cinders. Because of this, her two stepsisters began calling her Cinderella. They pointed their fingers and laughed at her, never realizing that with all their finery, they were not half as beautiful as the poor girl in the ashes.

• • •

This story may be the best-known fairy tale in the world. There are over 500 versions in Europe alone, and the tale has been told from China to Peru. In fact, the story of a girl cheated of her rightful place and made to be a servant to her stepmother and sisters has been popular for well over 1,200 years.

Whether it is called "Yeh-hsien" in China, "Rashin Coatie" in Scotland, "Aschenputtel" in Germany, or "Katie Woodencloak," "Mosseycoat," or "Donkeyskin," it has certainly earned its place in the storytelling world.

Now it happened that the king's son gave a great ball and everyone who was anyone in society was invited, including Cinderella's stepmother and stepsisters. So on top of all her other chores, Cinderella now had to iron their new dresses and touch up the laces and clean their diamonds and shine their silver baubles.

As she was helping the sisters into their gowns and combing their hair, one of them said, "Cinderella, I wager you would like to go to the ball," while the other laughed at the thought.

Of course Cinderella longed to go, but how could she? She had neither dress nor shoes, nor coach to take her. So when they all left, in a flurry of finery, in a coach pulled by four matched horses, she waved sadly, then went back into the house and sat down by the fire to weep.

She cried, "If only I could go to the ball, I should never ask for anything more."

Suddenly, her godmother, who was a fairy–with wings and a wand and who knew a wish when she heard it–appeared before her, wrapped in stars. "Will you work for your wish, my dear?"

Cinderella scrubbed away the tears with the back of her hand, and nodded.

"Then go into the garden and get me a pumpkin," said her fairy godmother.

Gladly, Cinderella did as she was asked and when she returned, the fairy had her scoop out the insides of the pumpkin. When that was done, the fairy touched the pumpkin with her wand and it turned into a splendid coach, gilded all over.

Then Cinderella was sent to the mousetrap where she found six gray mice and her fairy godmother struck each one in turn and they became grey horses to pull the coach.

"But what shall we do for a coachman?" mused the fairy.

"I know where there's a rat in the rat-trap," said Cinderella and quickly went to fetch him, and he became a round, jolly coachman.

Then six green lizards were found who became footmen, their liveries as green as their skins had been.

"Get in, get in," cried the fairy, "there's no time to waste."

"But I cannot go dressed like this," Cinderella pointed out sensibly, "for I should never be let in."

So her godmother touched the wand to Cinderella's raggedy dress and it turned into cloth of gold and silver, with loops of diamonds and pearls cunningly worked along the bodice and hem. Right after that, the godmother touched Cinderella's bare feet and she was suddenly shod in glass slippers, as fine as any shoe in the most elegant shop.

"Now go and dance until midnight," said the fairy, "but be certain you leave when the bells strike the hour, for the magic will fail at the last stroke and you will have only a pumpkin, six mice, six lizards, and a rat to bring you home."

The three elements in all the Cinderella stories are: the girl deprived of her inheritance, the help of a magic maker, and the girl not allowed to reveal herself until she is recognized. In most tales there is no glass slipper; indeed in some there is no slipper at all. A few scholars feel that the glass slipper was a mistake on the part of either Charles Perrault, who set the tale down in French, or one of his translators, who mistook the word vair, *which means variegated fur, for* verre, *which means glass.*

Cinderella promised, "Oh I will, Godmother, I will," and away she went.

• • •

When she got to the ball, Cinderella looked like a magnificent foreign princess. No one knew her. The prince himself led her into the hall and danced only with her. He was about to give her a kiss and tell her he wanted to marry her when the clock in the bell tower began striking midnight.

Suddenly remembering what would happen at the last stroke, Cinderella tore herself away from the prince. She ran out of the castle and down the stairs. As she reached the gate, the last bell tolled and her coach was gone, her dress in tatters. The guards who let her out thought she was some country maid who had gotten in by mistake. And all that was left behind was one of the glass slippers, which the prince found.

• • •

Now when the stepsisters got home, they could only talk about the beautiful princess. Cinderella asked them to tell her more and, little suspecting, they did.

The next day, the prince sent around his royal coach with the glass slipper on a little pink cushion. He insisted that his valet let every young woman in the kingdom try the slipper on. "For I mean to marry the girl this glass slipper fits," he proclaimed.

So one by one the young women tried–big feet and little feet, fat feet and skinny feet–but the glass slipper fit none of them.

At last the prince's coach stopped before Cinderella's house. The two stepsisters tried on the shoes, but one had toes that were too big and one had a heel that was too large and neither could shove a foot into the slipper.

"Pray, let me try," begged Cinderella.

The two stepsisters laughed, but the valet pushed them aside. "My prince demands *every* young woman try," he said.

"She is just a cinder-maid," they protested, but the prince's valet insisted.

Of course, when he put the glass slipper on her foot, it went on with ease. The stepsisters were stunned, but even more stunned when Cinderella pulled the matching slipper from her pocket.

At that very moment, the fairy godmother appeared–wing, wand, and stars–and touched Cinderella's dress with magic, and suddenly she was even more magnificent than she had been at the ball.

Stepsisters and stepmother threw themselves at Cinderella's feet and begged for forgiveness and–for all the right reasons and none of the wrong ones–she did just that. Then she was escorted to the palace where the prince married her. Two days later, her stepsisters were married to two great lords of the court. And everyone really did live happily ever after. ★

Pumpkin Tartlets

What else would you do after midnight with a retired coach?

(Makes 40 tartlets)

Facts about pumpkins:
1. The word pumpkin comes from the Greek word pepon, *meaning large melon. (Indeed, it is not a vegetable, but a fruit.)*
2. Pumpkins originated in Central America, perhaps as far back as 5500 BCE. *The Native Americans ate pumpkin long before the Pilgrims landed.*
3. Pumpkins are healthy and contain potassium, beta-carotene, and Vitamin A. Once they were used as a cure for freckles and snakebite.

EQUIPMENT:

- bowl
- can opener
- mixing spoon
- measuring cup
- measuring spoons
- food processor
- mini muffin pan
- 3-inch round cookie cutter or a drinking glass
- paper towel
- toothpick

INGREDIENTS:

Filling:

- 1 15-oz. can of pumpkin (450 g)
- ½ cup evaporated milk (115 ml)
- 2 eggs
- ½ cup brown sugar (100 g)
- ½ cup sugar (100 g)
- 1 tsp. cinnamon
- ¼ tsp. ginger
- ¼ tsp. ground cloves
- ¼ tsp. nutmeg

Topping:

- ¼ cup ground walnuts (40 g)
- ¼ cup brown sugar (50 g)
- 1 tbsp. cold butter (12 g)

Crust:

- 4 pre-made pie crusts
- Butter to grease the muffin pan if it is not non-stick

Directions:

1. Preheat oven to 425 degrees F (220 C).

2. Mix all the filling ingredients in a bowl. Set aside.

3. Grind walnuts in the food processor. Add the brown sugar and butter cut into small pieces. Grind until crumbly.

4. If your mini muffin pan is not non-stick, butter the insides or spray lightly with cooking spray.

5. Lay out the pie crusts and cut them into rounds by placing the cookie cutter or drinking glass upside down and pushing down firmly. You should be able to get approximately 10 tartlet shells from each pie shell. They do not need to be perfectly round.

6. Gently press the rounds into the muffin tin. This is easier if you form them into a slight cup shape first so you don't poke a hole through them.

7. Put 1 tablespoon filling in each shell.

8. Sprinkle with 1 teaspoon of the topping.

9. Put the tartlets in the oven for 10 minutes.

10. With the tartlets still in the oven, lower the temperature to 350 degrees F (175 C) and cook for 12–15 more minutes or until a toothpick can be stuck in and comes out clean.

11. Cool for 5–10 minutes before removing from the tin.

4. The largest pumpkin ever grown weighed 1,140 pounds.
5. The largest pumpkin pie ever baked weighed over 350 pounds (160 kg). It used 80 pounds (36 kg) of cooked pumpkin and took six hours to bake.
6. Pumpkins are 90 percent water.

The Magic Pear Tree

Long ago in China, a farmer brought his pears to the market in a hand-drawn cart. He was just setting up his stall when a Taoist priest, worn with care, came over to him.

"Please," said the priest, "may I have a piece of fruit. Just one old, bruised pear will do, I do not ask for more."

The farmer tried to get rid of him, but the priest would not leave. He held out his hand, begging for that one pear.

"I sell my fruit, I do not give them away," said the farmer angrily. "I do not like beggars, whether they are priests or poor men. Away with you."

Soon, of course, this argument drew a crowd. The crowd drew the guards. And finally, to disperse the crowd, one of the guards purchased a small pear and threw it to the priest.

This story of magic is from late seventeenth-century China. The Taoist priest who conjures up the pear tree has probably, like the Taoist priests of his era, studied a combination of alchemy, astrology, botany, zoology, and of course, the martial arts.

These priests often lived in the mountains of China. Followers of the Tao, they believed in deep contemplation and a non-aggressive approach to life.

Though Taoism had been around for many centuries, it didn't become a recognized religion in China until the second century CE.

The priest nodded and thanked the guard, then spoke to the crowd. "How hard it is to understand greed. Let me offer some pears to all of you. All I wanted was a seed for planting." He ate the pear but reserved the seed.

Now the people crowded around to see what he would do next.

Taking a little shovel that he had tied around his back, the priest dug a hole and planted the seed, covering it up with earth.

"Can someone bring me hot water?"

A cautious laugh ran around the crowd, but one small boy ran, got the water, and gave it to the priest who immediately poured it on the planted seed.

Suddenly a green shoot shot up from the dark earth. It grew and grew and grew some more until it became an enormous pear tree, bursting with blooms. Even as the people watched, the blooms became pears, golden and heavy.

The priest turned, plucked the pears, and distributed them to everyone in the crowd, saving two for the small boy who had run for the water.

Then taking his shovel, the priest chopped down the tree. When he was finished, he picked up the top half of the tree and walked down the road. The people watched until he was out of sight.

Immediately the crowd dispersed and the farmer, who had been watching all of this magical show with them, turned back to his cart to find it was entirely empty and the handle of his wagon had been chopped off as well.

"Hey!" he cried, looking around. But priest, handle, guards, crowd–and pears–were all gone and he was left with nothing. ✮

Today, most people in the West would recognize Taoist priests from such Hong Kong movies as Crouching Tiger, Hidden Dragon.

The Chinese philosopher Lao-Tzu (c.604–521 BCE*), summed up its tenets thus:*

Look, and it can't
be seen.
Listen, and it can't
be heard.
Reach, and it can't
be grasped.

Magic Pear Grumble

Cures the grumbling of even the hungriest belly. And the secret ingredient? Hot water to make it grow. (Serves a family)

Facts about pears:
1. Pears have been part of the Asian diet for centuries. They traveled to Europe in the Middle Ages, and to America in 1620.
2. In the eighteenth century, pears were nicknamed "butter fruit" because of their soft texture.
3. The pear is actually a member of the rose family.

EQUIPMENT:

- large bowl
- measuring cup
- measuring spoons
- whisk
- peeler
- knife
- small heat-proof bowl
- teakettle or pan to boil water
- rubber spatula
- 2-quart (2 liter) baking dish or casserole

INGREDIENTS:

- 1 cup flour (115 g)
- ⅔ cup sugar (265 g)
- 1½ tsp. baking powder
- ½ tsp. cinnamon
- ⅛ tsp. salt
- ⅛ tsp. ground cloves
- ½ cup milk (115 ml)
- 4 ripe pears, peeled, cored, and cut into ½–¾ inch (1–2 cm) chunks
- ¾ cup packed light brown sugar (150 g)
- ¼ cup butter (55 g), cut into 5 pieces
- ¾ cup boiling water (175 ml)

DIRECTIONS:

1. Preheat the oven to 375 degrees F (190 C).

2. In the large bowl, using the whisk, mix together the flour, white sugar, baking powder, cinnamon, salt, and ground cloves until completely combined.

3. Add milk and beat until smooth. This batter will be very thick and sticky.

4. With the rubber spatula, fold in the pear chunks.

5. Scoop the batter into the ungreased baking dish or casserole.

6. Boil water and measure ¾ cup (175 ml). (If you put the correct amount of water on to boil, it will be less when it is hot.)

7. Put the butter and brown sugar into the small heat-proof bowl and pour the hot water over it. Stir until melted and blended.

8. Pour the hot water mixture over the batter in the baking dish/casserole–do not mix.

9. Bake for 45 minutes. The finished dessert will be still a little syrupy with golden brown bready tufts.

4. Of the more than 3,000 varieties of pears, the most popular is the Bartlett.
5. Pears are a healthy snack and a good source of Vitamin C and fiber.
6. Pears ripen better off the tree than on. Some experts even recommend putting them in a brown paper bag and leaving them at room temperature, to hasten ripening.

Snow White

Once in midwinter, the snow falling like feathers from the sky, a queen sat by her bedchamber window embroidering a piece of cloth. The frame of the window was dark ebony, night-black. The snow was an unblemished white. The queen accidentally pricked her finger with the needle and three drops of blood landed on the snow.

Time seemed to stop, the world ceased turning, the queen sighed. "I wish I had a child as white as snow, as red as blood, as black as wood."

Nine months later she gave birth to a daughter who was white as snow, with blood-red lips, and hair as black as ebony. Her father called her Snow White.

But when the child was born, the queen died, and all that followed was a consequence of wishing.

• • •

Worried that his daughter needed a mother and the kingdom needed a queen, the king married a year later. The woman was beautiful, but she was proud, haughty, cold as ice. She was an enchantress whose magic mirror spoke to her in the dead of the night.

Often the new queen would look in the mirror and say:

"Mirror, mirror, on the wall,
Who's the fairest of us all?"

1. The main written source of this tale can be found in the Grimm's collection. The Grimm brothers got the tale from two sisters, Jeannette and Amalie Hassenpflug of Cassel.
2. The story has appeared with little variation from the British Isles to Asia Minor and even into Central Africa.
3. Earlier literary versions of the story can be found in Il Pentamerone, *an Italian collection of stories, but they were never as popular as the Grimm tale.*

And the mirror would grow cloudy, then sharp, and reply:

"Answering you by your own demand–
You are the fairest in the land."

But Snow White was growing up, and she was a beautiful child. More beautiful, many said, than the queen.

• • •

One day when Snow White had turned thirteen years old, the queen asked her mirror the same question:

"Mirror, mirror, on the wall,
Who's the fairest of us all?"

This time the mirror grew cloudy, then sharp, and replied:

"That you are beautiful, queen, 'tis true,
But Snow White is much more beautiful than you."

The queen screamed and threw her hairbrush at the mirror. Luckily her aim was terrible and she hit the window instead, shattering it. She could not, however, as easily break the memory of what the mirror had said. Day and night, envy had her by the throat and gnawed at her.

At last she called her best huntsman to her.

"Take the child, Snow White, into the woods. Kill her and bring me her heart and liver as proof of what you have done."

The huntsman was terrified. "She is the king's daughter, majesty."

The queen drew herself up and her face was both beautiful and terrible at the same time. "I am the king's wife."

• • •

The huntsman knew that he had to obey. He went to Snow White and said he was to take her hunting. And eager to learn, Snow White went away with him.

But when they were in the deepest part of the forest, the huntsman drew his knife. "I am only obeying the queen's command, princess," he said.

"Oh huntsman, spare my life," Snow White cried, looking up at him with limpid eyes. "I shall run into the forest and never return."

He put away the knife. "Run away, child, run away!" And as soon as she was gone, he killed a young deer and cut out its heart and liver and brought it back to the wicked queen. He told her they belonged to the child.

The queen had the cook salt and cook the meat and ate it, savoring every bite.

• • •

Meanwhile in the woods, Snow White ran desperately on and on, over sharp stones, through sharper thorns, and into the dark of night. At last, exhausted, and cold, and frightened beyond measure, she came upon a little cottage in the woods. Without even knocking she went in and to her surprise the place was as neat and clean as a palace.

The table was set with seven places, and there were seven little beds neatly made at the back of the room. She tried one bed after

4. In 1937, Walt Disney made a movie version of the story, basing it on the Grimm's telling, though he left out the ending where the witch must dance in red-hot iron shoes.

5. Snow White and the Seven Dwarfs *was the first commercially successful TechniColor feature-length animated film. Until the Disney movie, the seven dwarfs did not have names or distinct personalities.*

another, but they were either too short or too long, too hard or too soft. At last, she crept onto the seventh bed and as it was just right, she fell fast asleep.

Not a minute later, the owners of the cottage came home. They were seven dwarfs who worked the mines. They looked around the house, smelling a strange human smell. And when they found Snow White, small and beautiful, they let her sleep. The seventh dwarf shared a bed one hour at a time with each of his companions until night was done.

• • •

In the morning, Snow White awoke and found the little men awake before her. She told them of her troubles and how her wicked stepmother had tried to have her killed.

The little men said, “Stay here with us. We will protect you and you can be our sister. Keep the house neat while we work and have hot supper ready for us when we return and all will be well. But be sure never to let anyone come in while we are away.”

“With all my heart,” cried Snow White.

And so it was.

• • •

Now the queen, believing that she had eaten Snow White’s heart and liver, went to the mirror. And she asked gaily:

“Mirror, mirror, on the wall,
Who’s the fairest of us all?”

The mirror grew cloudy, then sharp, and replied:

“You are beautiful, queen, ’tis true,
But Snow White in the forest is more beautiful than you.”

"Snow White? She is dead!" cried the queen.

The mirror answered:

"Over the hill, where seven dwarfs dwell
Snow White still lives, beautiful and well."

The queen knew this had to be true, for the mirror was incapable of lying. So she had the huntsman put in the dungeon for deceiving her. Then she took out her basket of magical potions. She drank down one after another until she looked like a young peddler woman. In this disguise she went into the forest to find the house of the seven dwarfs.

The little cottage was neat and snug. Lights gleamed from the window. The peddler woman knocked on the door. "I have laces," she cried. "Pretty laces."

When Snow White looked out the window and saw her, she had no fear and invited the young woman in.

"May I try on the laces?" she asked.

"Of course, my pretty," said the peddler woman, but she laced Snow White up so tightly, the girl could not breathe and fell down as if dead.

"Now I am the most beautiful," said the wicked queen with a laugh, and she raced home to the palace.

• • •

Not long after the dwarfs returned home, found Snow White, and cut the laces. As soon as Snow White returned to life again, she told them what had happened.

"That was no peddler–that was your stepmother in disguise," they said. "Never let anyone into the house."

Snow White promised, "With all my heart."

And so it was.

• • •

But the queen, back in her palace, soon asked the mirror her question and was returned the same reply.

"You are beautiful, queen, 'tis true,
But Snow White in the forest is more beautiful than you."

What could she do but haul out her potions again. This time she disguised herself as a middle-aged peddler woman and carried with her a poisoned comb.

When she arrived at the cottage, and knocked at the door, Snow White looked out the window. "I cannot let you in."

"Then you come out, dearie," said the peddler woman. And, as Snow White had not been warned against that, she did.

"Let me comb your hair and you will see how lovely this golden comb looks against your dark hair," said the peddler.

But no sooner had Snow White agreed, then the poison began its deadly work and in moments the girl lay senseless on the ground.

“Now I am the most beautiful,” said the wicked queen with a laugh, and she raced home to the palace.

Fortunately it was almost dinner time and the dwarfs arrived home, took out the comb, and Snow White was once again saved.

• • •

Meanwhile in the palace, the queen learned once again that Snow White was still alive for the mirror told her:

“Over the hill, where seven dwarfs dwell
Snow White still lives, beautiful and well.”

The queen shook with rage. She dragged out her basket of potions once more and drank down every one until she looked like an ancient crone. Taking a new fallen apple, green on one side, red on the other, she set a deadly poison in the red side but let the green side be. Then off she sped to the cottage with a basket full of apples, and the death-bearing one on the top.

This time Snow White was ever more cautious. “I cannot let you in, I cannot go outside.”

“You need to do neither, my pretty,” said the crone. “I just wish to give you my basket of apples so that you may cook seven little pies for your little men. And so you be not afraid of the apples, I will even eat of one.” And she took a big bite out of the green side of the top apple. “I will leave them here for you.” Then the old crone hobbled away.

• • •

As soon as she saw the old woman was away from the clearing, Snow White ventured outside. The apple, half eaten, looked so inviting–magic can tempt even the wary–that she picked it up and took a big bite of the red and luscious-looking side. The poisoned apple stuck in her throat and she fell down, dead.

The wicked queen came out from behind a tree where she had been hiding and she danced around the fallen girl. "Now I am the most beautiful." And with a laugh, she picked up the rest of the poisoned apple and raced home to the palace.

There she asked the mirror her question and the mirror answered:

"Answering you by your own demand–

You are the fairest in the land."

And the queen was satisfied at last.

• • •

When the dwarfs came home that evening and found Snow White lying cold and stiff on the ground, they could not find how she was poisoned, for they could not see the apple piece in her throat.

They were going to bury her, but she looked so beautiful–white and red and black–that they could not bear to shut her away in the earth. So they made a glass casket and set her at the crossroads with a sign marked with golden letters:

SHE IS A KING'S DAUGHTER AND A FRIEND.

• • •

Now it happened that a king's son had come through the woods with his hunting party and he found the glass casket and read the sign. And when he looked through the glass, Snow White was so beautiful and innocent that he fell in love right then.

"Let me take the casket home," he begged the dwarfs. "I will prize her above all others for the rest of my life."

So the dwarfs let him take the casket away but as his servants began lifting it, one of them stumbled over a tree stump. The bump jarred the bit of poisoned apple, which fell out of Snow White's mouth and with a sigh she lifted the lid of the coffin and sat up.

"Where am I?" she asked in wonder.

"With the man who loves you truly," replied the young prince.

• • •

So Snow White went with the prince to the kingdom across the mountain and became his bride.

Now the wicked stepmother and her husband the king were invited to the wedding, though they did not know who the bride was. The evil queen arrayed herself in her finest clothes and stood in front of her mirror and asked:

"Mirror, mirror, on the wall,
Who's the fairest of us all?"

The mirror grew cloudy, then sharp, and replied:

"You are beautiful, 'tis true,
But the new young queen is more beautiful than you."

The wicked woman could not believe this and went on to the wedding. When she got there, she recognized Snow White, and turned to leave, but it was too late. They had been waiting for her to arrive and the guards grabbed her by the arms and forced her into red hot iron slippers, which she had to dance in until she dropped down dead. ★

Snow White's Baked Apples

The fairest dessert of all. (Serves one person per apple)

Facts about apples:
1. The apple was the most popular fruit of ancient Greeks and Romans. There is evidence of humans eating apples as early as 6500 BCE. The Romans probably introduced apples to much of Europe.
2. The science of apple growing is called pomology. There are now 7,500 varieties of apples grown throughout the world.
3. Apples are members of the rose family.

EQUIPMENT:

- sharp knife
- fruit coring tool or a thin sharp knife
- cutting board
- small bowl
- measuring cup
- measuring spoons
- butter knife
- baking pan

INGREDIENTS:

- 1 apple per person, any kind, though red-skinned varieties hold up better
- ¼ cup sugar (50 g)
- 1 tbsp. cinnamon
- 1 heaping tbsp. raisins per apple
- 1 tbsp. butter per apple
- Juice: orange, apple, apple cider, or cranberry

DIRECTIONS:

1. Preheat oven to 350 degrees F (175 C).

2. Mix the cinnamon and sugar together in a small bowl.

3. Cut off the top and bottom of each apple–just a thin slice.

4. Core each apple, either by pushing the coring tool straight through the middle or by carefully cutting it out with a thin sharp knife. Make sure not to leave any seeds.

5. Place the apple(s) in the baking dish.

6. Layer the following into each apple: some of the raisins, some of the butter, then a bit of the cinnamon sugar. Pack each down a bit with a clean finger and repeat. Finish off with cinnamon sugar around the exposed part of the apple. Do not put raisins outside the apple as they will burn.

7. Pour a ¼ inch (1 cm) of juice into the bottom of the pan.

8. Bake uncovered 70 to 90 minutes. Serve with ice cream.

VARIATIONS:

Try the following instead of, or in addition to, the basic recipe: Dried cranberries, dried cherries, white raisins, maple syrup, brown sugar, ground cloves and nutmeg (only a little of these), or walnuts.

4. It takes apple trees four to five years to produce their first fruit. The apples may range from cherry size to ones as large as grapefruit.
5. There is no fat, sodium, or cholesterol in apples, though a medium apple has about 80 calories. Apples are also a good source of fiber and vitamin C, iron, and phosphates.
6. Modern doctors have discovered that apples can help reduce high cholesterol, soften gallstones, reduce fever, help prevent heart disease and cancer, and aid digestion.